# Original Orik and His Important Job

Written by Chris Engstrom

Illustrated by Dimpple Koul



Published by M&B Global Solutions, Inc.

# Dedication

For the Graham family, who raised the most intelligent, loving and persistent pup. And for Jack Nigl, Susan Elliot, Sue Robinson and all the members of Northeast Wisconsin Service Dogs, who never gave up on us and provided so many people a way to fight for their dreams.

**What's that noise? Does Christy need me?**
**"Orik, get the slippers," Christy says tiredly.**

As the sun comes up, I stretch my legs and wag my tail. It is time for my person, Christy, to get up and into her wheelchair. We have lots to do!

"Good morning, Orik. How are you today?" Christy says with a cheery tone. "I'll feed you in a minute.Just wait." Wait? But I'm hungry now! Sometimes humans just don't understand.

I'm good at ignoring food at resturants, but this is our house.
Can I please have just a little bite of that muffin?
"Orik, this is mine," Christy says "You will get yours. Be patient."

Christy and I do lots of fun things together. I get to go wherever she goes. That's because I'm a very smart dog! Dogs like me are called service dogs. In the morning after she wakes up, Christy has to get ready to go to work. I have a job, too.

My job is to help Christy. Her muscles don't move like other people. We go everywhere together! Going places and seeing people is so exciting. Learning how to be a good service dog was not easy.

When I was a puppy, I lived with a family that brought me to classes and worked with me at home so I could learn how to help someone like Christy. Every week I learned new things. The teachers were very nice and taught us things that we could do to practice every day. It was hard work, but I like being a smart dog. Everyone said that I was special because I did good work and loved being around people.

Once Christy and I were matched as a team, we had to learn how to work together. That was the hardest job of all! Christy's body moves differently and her voice doesn't sound anything like my other teachers. Everything was new and different. The teachers had to come to our house and help us a lot.

"We will do this, Orik. I believe in you," Christy would say. Even though it was very challenging, we worked hard every day and never gave up. Christy wanted me to be her dog with all her heart! She knew we would be a great team. Now, I can do all sorts of things to help Christy.

In the morning after Christy is up, it's time for me to get dressed and eat my breakfast. When I'm dressed, I have to be very calm and respond to Christy when she needs me. I wear a vest that shows people I am a service dog. The vest reminds me to pay attention and tells people not to distract me. My vest says DO NOT PET. If people touch me, then I forget that I need to work. When I get excited, I get silly and bark! Service dogs aren't allowed to make noise in public. Christy needs my help. I play when done working and when Christy says it's okay.

I also wear a head collar called a gentle leader. The leader helps me follow Christy's wheelchair. It doesn't hurt at all. It's my steering wheel.

When I'm dressed in my vest, we can go out in public. The bus takes us anywhere we need to go. I usually lie down and take a rest while riding the bus. It's hard to ignore all the people and sounds, but Christy says I do a great job staying calm.

I push the button at Christy's office so we can go through the door by ourselves.

Inside, I rest and wait for Christy to call me.
After a while, I hear her say, "Orik, get the pen."
I'm glad I can help.

Sometimes I'm so happy that I want to play, but I have to wait until Christy gets her work done. If I do a good job, I get a treat, hugs and kisses! "Thank you for not petting Orik when he is working," Christy tells people. When it's time to leave, I sometimes say hello. The people in the office love giving me attention.

We go to the grocery store a few times each week. "Please don't pet him when he is working," Christy reminds people. Today, I held our wallet and gave the woman at the register our money so we could pay for the groceries.
DO NOT PET
SERVICE DOG

As we were leaving, I smelled fresh, juicy food. Yum, those are my favorites. "Orik you are ALWAYS hungry!" Christy giggles."You have got to be the hungriest dog in the whole world! Leave it alone. Those are for when we get home, silly." It's tough to ignore food that smells so good. Even though it's hard, I have to listen to Christy. Dogs aren't allowed to eat in the grocery store, not even service dogs like me.

In the parking lot, a family stopped Christy to ask questions about me. They asked how I help her and were amazed at how I can pick up the keys so easily! She explained that service dogs are very nice, but it's important to ask the person before touching us. When I'm doing a very hard job, I need to focus on being calm and helping Christy. That's okay, because I love to work with her. Christy is my favorite person in the whole world. It makes me very proud that I can help her.

**Since we were done shopping and out in the parking lot, Christy said I could "shake" hands. It's fun teaching people what I can do.**

When we get home, I turn on the light and bring Christy the remote control.

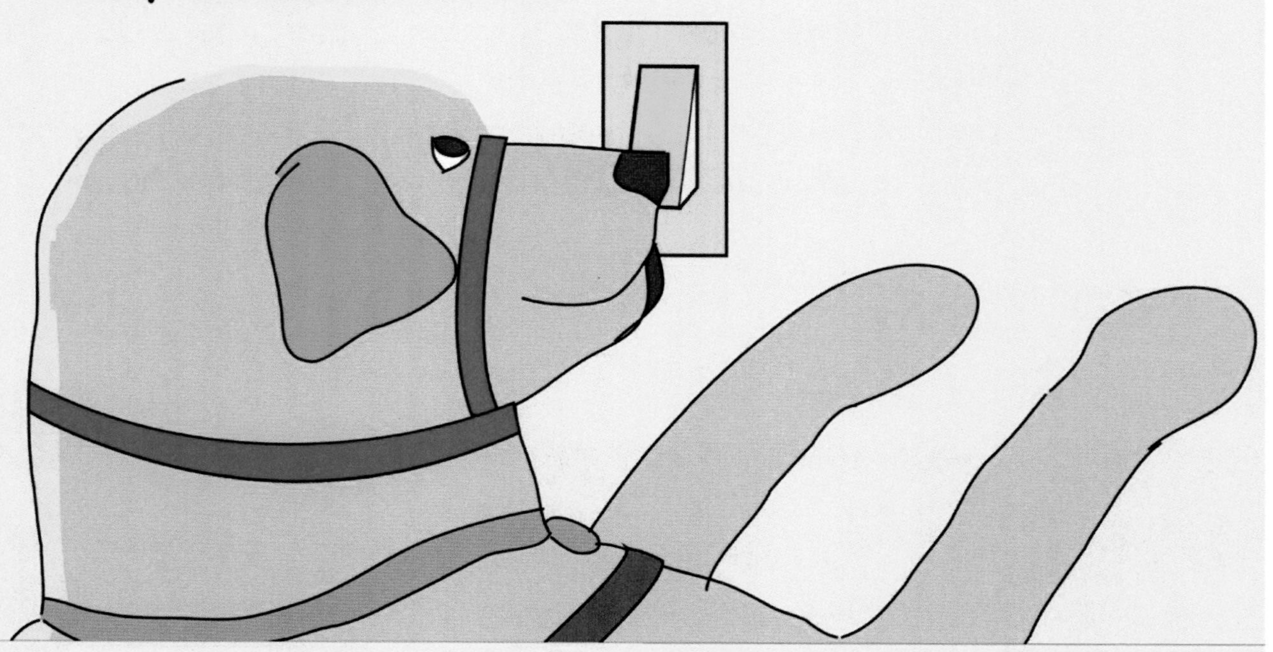

Then I take off my vest and leader.

Time to play! I love chasing my ball and toys when I'm done with my work. I get to run, jump, and tug all I want. Fetch is my favorite game! WOOF WOOF WOOF! WOOF WOOF! Hurry up, Christy. Throw it! Bet you can't catch me. WOOF WOOF WOOF! "That's enough, Orik. Easy!" Christy says. "You can be silly, but not so loud, you goofy boy." I have a really hard time being quiet when I'm excited. Playing makes me happy!

For dinner tonight, I got an extra special treat put in my food. I love the smell of apples and carrots.

When I finished eating, Christy told me to open the refrigerator so she could get her food. The turkey sandwich smelled so good! "Leave it, Orik. That's not yours," she said.

Christy told me to wait while she washed her hands. All I could smell was the yummy sandwich sitting on the counter. I know it's hers, but I just wanted a tiny bite. Before I knew it, the plate was on the floor and the sandwich was in my belly.

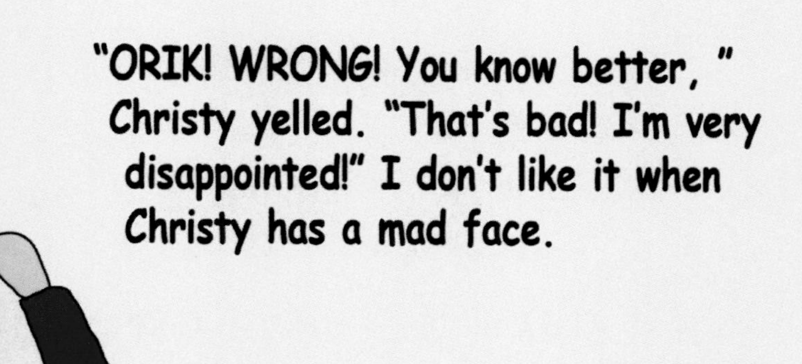

"ORIK! WRONG! You know better, " Christy yelled. "That's bad! I'm very disappointed!" I don't like it when Christy has a mad face.

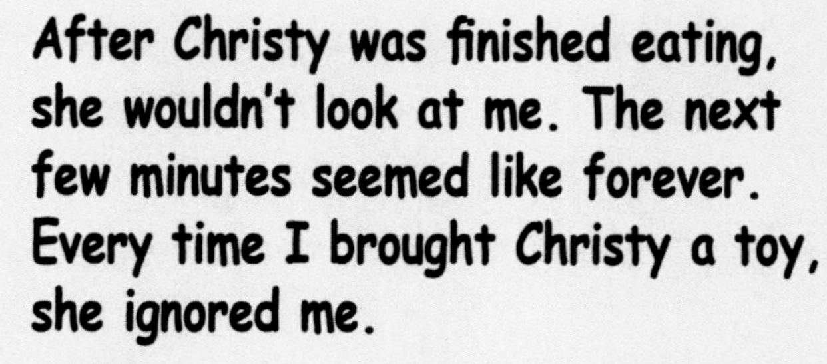

After Christy was finished eating, she wouldn't look at me. The next few minutes seemed like forever. Every time I brought Christy a toy, she ignored me.

Then something great happened! I heard Christy say, "Orik, come." Is it time to play again? "Look, Orik. Find the phone." Phone – I know what that is! I searched everywhere around our house. Where could she have left it?

Not on the desk ...
Not on the counter ...
Not in the sink ...

Not under the bed ...

Not on the couch ...

Is it in the closet?

There's the phone! I found it! Christy was so proud of me that she gave me a big hug and kiss.

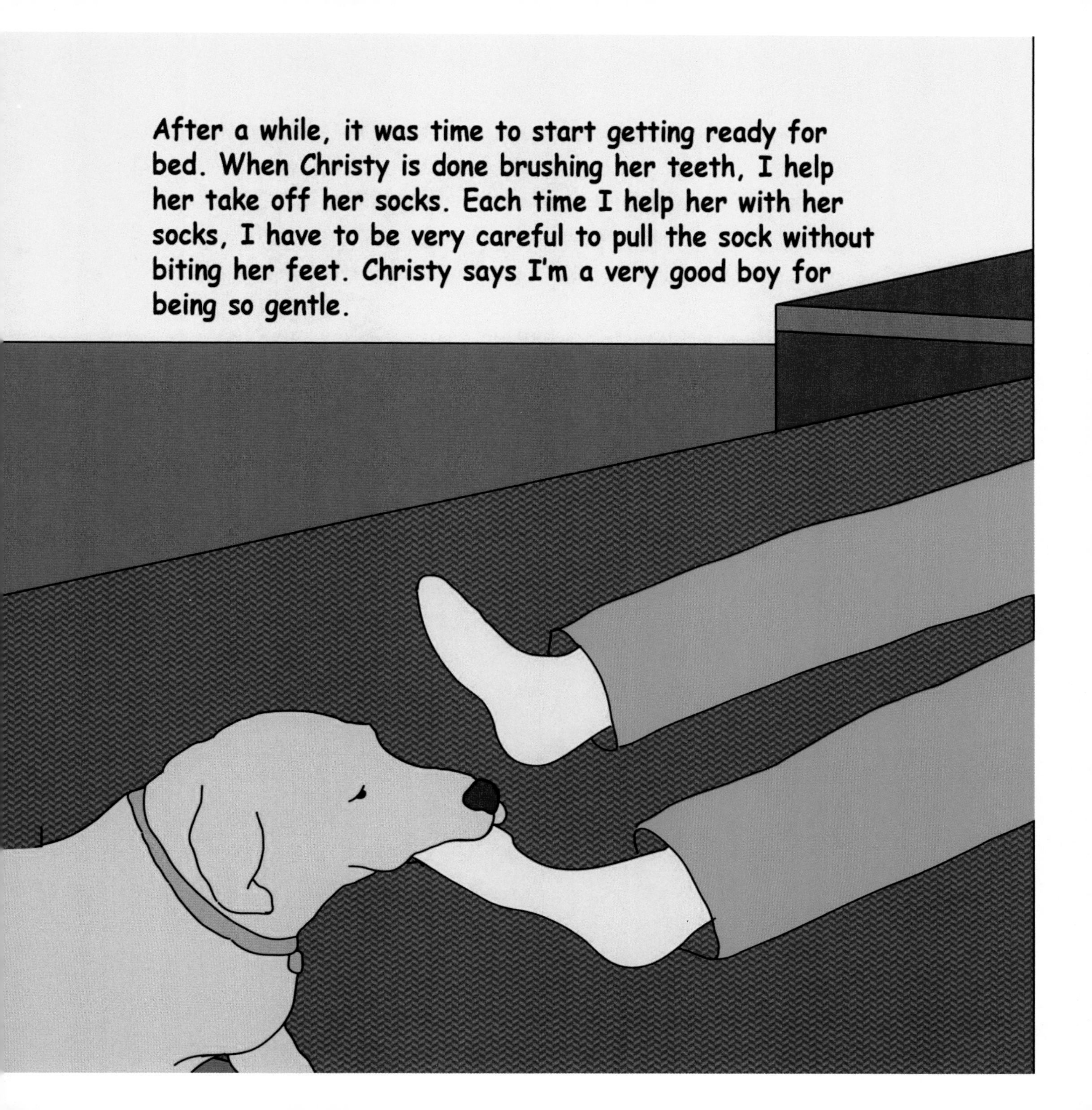

After a while, it was time to start getting ready for bed. When Christy is done brushing her teeth, I help her take off her socks. Each time I help her with her socks, I have to be very careful to pull the sock without biting her feet. Christy says I'm a very good boy for being so gentle.

Once she is in bed,I get to cuddle with her. "Nobody is perfect, not even a service dog like you," Christy says."There is only one Orik. You are original and unique.That's why I love you, Big O."

I like having a special job,but I love my person, Christy, the most! I help her and she loves me.That's all a dog can ask for.

## Acknowledgements

I would like to thank my publishers, Bonnie Groessl and Mike Dauplaise of M&B Global Solutions, for their tireless work and dedication in bringing this project to life.

Thank you to my supporters who backed this project from the beginning and gave me the encouragement I needed to move forward.

I would like to thank my family for teaching me what it means to be dedicated and determined to reach a goal. I would also like to thank members of my Green Bay family who are there for me in good times and bad.

## About the Author

Chris Engstrom lives independently with cerebral palsy in Green Bay, Wisconsin, with her faithful service dog, Orik. Chris double-majored in psychology and human development at the University of Wisconsin-Green Bay, where she participated as a student manager for the women's basketball program.

Chris is a member of the Psi Chi National Honor Society in Psychology and is pursuing a master's degree in school counseling. She also works for the Green Bay YMCA's 21C At-Risk After School Program in partnership with the Green Bay Area Public School District, where she assists students with their social and emotional development.

Made in the USA
Middletown, DE
09 December 2022